The Covewae Cookbook

An amazing menu of ridiculous meals

by

Richard Digance

About The Author

Richard Digance is a BAFTA Nominated entertainer and a proud recipient of The Gold Award from The British Academy of Composers and Songwriters. He is also one of just a handful of folksinger/songwriters listed in The Virgin Anthology of Songwriters.

Born in West Ham, London, in 1949, and although having never attended a class reunion, he attended Vicarage Lane Primary School, East Ham and then Thomas Lethaby Secondary Modern, before attending college in East Ham, London and Glasgow until he chose creative arts over the arduous task of studying.

His TV career spanned 17 years, culminating in his own ITV show for London Weekend Television, on which he played a guitar duet with Queen's Brian May, as well as playing with Status Quo and The Moody Blues. He also appeared in Dictionary Corner on Channel 4s Countdown nearly 200 times.

On the comedy front he supported movie legend Steve Martin in America and the legendary Robin Williams at The London Palladium, the world-famous theatre where he also supported Roy Orbison and even tuned the legend's sacred red guitar.

He developed from playing folk clubs when a student to the theatre stage, first as a support act in the 1970s before becoming a headline act in his own right. During that decade he learnt his trade as an inter-acting entertainer by supporting Jethro Tull, Supertramp, Steeleye Span, Joan Armatrading, Elkie Brooks, Chas and Dave, The Kinks, David Essex and Tom Jones on their British tours. In just one year, 1977, he performed as a support act 285 times.

He has also composed audiobook soundtracks and songs for Bill Bryson, the world's best-selling travel writer and has ghost-written various books and after-dinner speeches for celebrities in sport, including the late football legend, George Best and cricket legend David Gower.

A successful author, Richard has published 20 books and his children's collection of verse, The Animal Alphabet, serialised by The BBC, is still used around the world in 15 different countries as an English teaching aid.

Some of the syllabus levels and publishers of Richard's work around the world include.

Fearon Teacher Aids Series, Grades 4-6, Illinois, USA.

The British Columbia Foundation Skills Assessment, University of British Columbia, Vancouver Canada.

The Canadian Ministry of Education website as part of their FSA tests since 2008

Oxford University Press Anthology of Verse.

The New Comprehensive Strategies 1-5, Book 3, The West Indies.

People For The Ethical Treatment of Animals (PETA) Foundation, London.

Western Australia Learning Aids, stages 1 & 2.

New Language For Learners, Form 1, Swaziland.

Richard also wrote and presented a musical for children, The War of The Worms, staged at The Newtown Theatre, as part of The Edinburgh Fringe Festival, starring alongside his daughter Rosie in a production that gained 5-star media reviews, including from The Stage.

Richard now lives a quieter life in the heart of the Wiltshire countryside, allowing him to reflect on great memories from a life well lived so far. Yet he has no intention to stop. It may seem strange but the 2021 lockdowns gave Richard the opportunity and impetus to re-evaluate his creative direction and thus concentrate more on writing than performing. This latest book of rather strange recipes and culinary hints is the result.

Disclaimer

Please note that no stones, blades of grass, twigs or any driftwood washed up on the shoreline of Covewae Island were injured or damaged in any way during the preparation of the ridiculous offerings throughout the pages of this book.

It should also be stated that Covewae Island cannot boast a single restaurant on the island so we have no idea what we are talking about in this book, so we insist you don't try any of our dishes. We totally accept they are complete rubbish, but hey, you bought this book, not us.

The Introduction

Welcome to, quite possibly, the most unique cookbook ever produced anywhere on our planet. A sweeping statement? You decide for yourself when you have browsed its pages.

You may well have purchased this book because you are fond of scrumptious food. That's obviously why people buy cookbooks, for the inspiration, the menus to try yourself. If that is the case, unlucky, this has been the worst investment you have ever made because you will probably not be tempted to emulate what is served up on Covewae Island when the dinner-bell sounds. You probably wouldn't touch these recipes with a bargepole. Actually, a bargepole may be far too big and cumbersome, but you definitely wouldn't be touching them with a chopstick.

The Covewae Cookbook is so different to all other cookery tomes, simply because none of the listed recipes within these pages are that enticing and certainly cannot be recommended to sensible people who love decent, traditional dishes that look and taste a pure delight.

On Cavewae Island food is nothing more than a contributor to survival as opposed to delicate, fancy dinner-party cuisine. It is based upon what is grown on its land or what swims around its shores. There is nothing to boast about here other than we can say with great confidence that all listings are successful ways of keeping alive, and we admit they are not so much mouth-watering as mouth-drying, so they are a good reason to enjoy a drink.

The big problem with creating such a book is the limitation of food varieties, which we can hardly be blamed for. The handful of sheep hanging around are treated more as pets as opposed to potential dinners.

With no supermarkets or shops on the island you would assume there are very few culinary choices, yet the island is surrounded by the world's biggest supermarket, the sea, a supermarket whose shelves are never empty.

So, under such circumstances, why compile a cookbook in the first place? A fair point, but everyone has to eat and, against all the odds, this is a truly inspiring collection that shows how to produce meals from items beyond the norm. Islanders need to use their imagination and they are delighted to share their ideas with readers such as yourself. Needs must, as they say, and the enclosed suggestions are wonderful ideas that will save money and lives.

Our head chef, who isn't really fond of cooking heads so may well be wrongly named, insists that cooking is nothing more than making food hotter than how it starts out, but due to a lack of amenities we have complied food selections that can be cooked on a bonfire or, should it be raining, served cold. Ok, that's a gross exaggeration as there is a fireplace in Rising Dale, the only residence on the island, so there are cooking facilities if not cooking skills.

Not all is lost as vegetables are grown in the kitchen garden and all food is as fresh as a daisy.

So, this is a book that can best be described as how the other half unfortunately live as opposed to how you should consider living yourself. It's a reference book more than an advisory manual or guide for the kitchen.

Having mentioned the bad points, we must now celebrate the master strokes that allow the inhabitants of the island to consume sufficient sustenance from things grown or found on Covewae.

The offerings are presented to you with pride and we hope its contents inspire you to try something new in your own kitchen. However, we will not be held responsible if you lose your friends in the process.

Preparing food can turn out to be a joke when attempted for the first time by those who never spend time in a kitchen. So, to prepare you for the looming pages, here are a few observations to get you in the mood.

Why do you never see broccoli in tins like peas or beans?

Why don't jellybeans grow to be jellies?

Why don't they make bigger tins for sardines?

Why is it only Guinness bubbles that sink? Fact.

Just a few smiles for starters, why questions that will now be followed by facts about food that maybe you didn't know.

Bananas contain so much potassium they are actually radioactive.

A tomato is actually a fruit and apples are a member of the rose family.

A potato is 80% water, just 10% less than a cucumber. Water is 100% water in case you didn't know.

Nan bread doesn't have to be baked by your grandmother.

It's cruel to spread a butterfly on a slice of bread.

You cannot pick your own strawberries if someone else has grown them.

Always keep an empty milk carton in the fridge just in case someone asks for a black coffee.

If a hen stares at a lettuce it's called a chicken Caesar salad.

A bagel is a doughnut with rigor-mortis.

With such strange ponderings it isn't surprising that cooking can be a time of confusion and that's why clever chef types write books, to help you with their suggestions. Sadly, you will soon discover that this cookery book will make things even more confusing. You have been warned.

Scanning the various courses you will soon discover how different our recipes are to other culinary ideas. The ideas within are gathered full knowing the lack of choice due to the small size of the island and a lack of available livestock. It isn't a case of vegetarian or non-vegetarian, or carnivores as they are known in official terms. After all, the island has been around longer than vegetarians. No-one seems to know when vegetarians were allowed in the country but it must have been long after the rock jutted out from The Atlantic Ocean. Hey, there's a pecking order in life and Covewae wins.

As an example, chickens can be seen on the island but they are not included in any menu for two reasons. Firstly, they roam free, as opposed to being caged, and can be difficult to catch as they jump around on slippery rocks, almost daring you to break your ankle. More importantly, there aren't too many of them and they are the only island's egg providers. Eggs are an important facet of any diet and if there were no chickens there would be no eggs. It's all about egg quality and not quantity or we'd or we'd all have ant farms, as they have the ability to produce ten thousand ants to every single hen's egg. In other words, that's why chickens are sacred island occupants and spared their freedom.

There were a few lambs at one point but they grew into sheep before we knew it and therefore not considered as foodstuff. Yes, the same can be said for Jasmine the goat, our milk provider. Goat milk consists of emulsified globules which means goat cream lasts longer than that which comes from cow's milk and it does not need to be homogenised. Goat milk contains just 3 to 4% fat and is therefore a healthy alternative to what the milkman would deliver, even if the island actually had a milk delivery from the mainland.

So be prepared for unfamiliar meals to follow your starter. Covewae Island has no chef, its menus are created by a survivor. Chefs worry about presentation of food whereas survivors concentrate more on essential goods, regardless of their appearance.

Contents

29. Grilled Grey Mullet
30. Breast of Shrimp
31. Undressed Crab
32. Sardines In Sauce
33. Peppered Sardines
34. Apple and Blackberry Pie
35. Corn On The Cod
36. T Bone Skate
37. Angel Fish Delight
38. Stuart's Pickled Onions
39. Wood Pigeon Pie
40. Sponges
41. Prawn Wellington
42. Beef Wellington
43. Turbot Dabs
44. Mushroom Soup
45. Interesting Food Facts
46. Clam Chops
47. Fish Thumbs
48. Hot Dogfish
49. Hop Scotch Eggs
50. Tossing The Conger
51. Covewae Paella
52. Crab Apple Sponge
53. Atlantic Roll
54. Butter Scotch
55. Battered Cod
56. Fishing Liners
57. Ravi-eel-i
58. Spratatouille

Prawn Cocktail

The Covewae prawn cocktail is very different to the bog standard prawn cocktail you will be served in a restaurant, mainly due to the salad dressing used. Instead of a thousand island dressing we use one island dressing.

There are over 900 islands off the coastline of Scotland so it's a country that's almost a salad dressing itself, not quite as mouth-watering as Indonesia but it deserves mention for its efforts. Ignore the fact that your One Island Dressing isn't pink as you may have expected, but more a greeny colour reminiscent of a stagnant pond, but don't let that put you off and stop you trying something different. Our One Island Dressing is to die for, and some have,

A meal for two.

Firstly, prepare the One Island dressing by mixing moss from waterside rocks with water. If you choose to use sea water, instantly available and therefore a sensible move, don't bother to add salt.

Place half a litre, approximately 1 pint, of water and boil it in a saucepan over an open fire. If the fire isn't open then find out what time it does open and wait.

Catch 12 prawns from the pool, fry slightly in sprat oil before placing in the saucepan and bringing to the boil.

When the prawns have cooled, apologise to them. They will understand.

Place the prawns on a bed of lettuce. They'll appreciate that.

If no lettuce is at hand then use the outer leaves of a cabbage or cauliflower. If you have none of these to hand use some grass.

Cover with the One Island dressing.

Crown with a sprig of parsley for no reason whatsoever.

Serve in a glass and if you cannot find spoons use scallop shells or any suitably shaped driftwood washed up on the shore.

This unique prawn cocktail is now ready for you and your guest to enjoy.

Gaelic Bread

A fine, unique delicacy, only found on Covewae Island. It doesn't taste anything like its French counterpart and will not give you bad breath the following morning, so it has everything going for it. The main difference is that garlic comes in cloves whereas the Gaelic came in rowing boats.

Bake a loaf of bread.

Cut the home-made loaf of bread into slices whilst you enjoy the wonderful smell that fills your kitchen.

So, what's the difference between an egg and a loaf of bread? You can beat an egg but you can't beat that smell a freshly baked loaf.

For health reasons, use a knife and not the saw you use for cutting hedges as it may contain remnants of spiders or ladybirds, both of which can cause violent indigestion for you and an even more savage outcome for them.

If preparing a romantic meal for two then bake a much smaller loaf to ensure the four slices, two each, will not be too thick. Delicacy is the name of the game here as a main course will follow.

Sprinkle with butter and shredded, freshly picked heather.

Place in a baking tray or on a flat rock.

Sprinkle sprat oil into the tray.

Place on a freshly lit bonfire to ensure the bread does not burn. With no oven gauge to assist, we suggest you use a fire that has not been alight more than 8 minutes.

Cook above the flames for 10 minutes.

Serve hot.

Failing that, serve cold.

To ensure you do not burn your hand when retrieving your Gaelic Bread from the fire, why not ask a friend to do it for you instead? Hey, what's a blister on a finger amongst friends.

A fantastic way to begin the most enjoyable of evenings with friends.

Scotch Mist Soup

The perfect winter starter to warm the cockles of any heart, although by all accounts it never warms the hearts of any cockles, so it's a bit of a one-way pleasure. Scotch Mist Soup is a derivative of the popular Scotch Broth Soup, so often seen in Scotland and in tins around Britain's supermarkets. The main difference between the two soups is that Scotch Mist Soup doesn't contain meat or numerous varieties of vegetables. It's more a soup of the night as opposed to a soup of the day.

Scotch Mist Soup can only be found on Covewae Island, all very well but nobody can find the island itself, so you must follow these directions carefully to get it right. With over 900 islands around the Scottish coastline it's difficult to know which is Covewae, if indeed it's one of the 900 anyway.

Scotch Mist Soup is best prepared during the hours of darkness.

Place an empty saucepan in your garden, or window-box if you don't have a garden.

Allow the mist to gather in the saucepan during the night.

Slice a carrot into little orange circles whilst you wait for mist to fall.

By the way, if rabbits love carrots and carrots help you see in the dark, how come so many of them get run over during the night? We move on.

Odd a sliced onion if you wish but not compulsory.

Place the saucepan on the open fire and bring mist to boil.

When mist is boiling, add carrots and possibly onions

Simmer for 10 minutes.

Serve with home-made bread.

Do not overcook or the carrots will turn to mush.

For more helpings put your saucepan out when thick fog.

The above recipe works a treat using overnight mist or fog but doesn't seem to be so successful when leaving your saucepan outside during a thunderstorm or a snowstorm. Too much liquid will dilute the exotic taste of the sliced carrots.

Scotch Mist is a popular soup
Inspired by Covewae's Scotch Mist
We go to the highest point on the island
That's how we add this soup to the list

We go to an area of land that's boggy
And sit and wait until it's foggy
When the fog and mist comes down
We scoop up all the moisture around

We take a bowl used for soup
And of course we will need a scoop
For this a scallop shell works well
If a ladle doesn't ring a bell

Then the soup bowl you take hold
And drink it down before it gets cold
A worthy meal to keep in the loop
Covewae Island's Scotch Mist Soup

Covewae Pate

Pate, in all its varieties, comes from all corners of Europe and is a popular starter in the most fashionable of restaurants, particularly in Belgium in general and Brussels in particular. Basically pate is nothing more than a lump of meat with a posh name. Some will say all pates taste the same, and those who disagree have to admit they all look fairly similar anyway, so much so it's a great way of getting rid of an old tin of corned beef that happens to be the longest-serving resident in your food cabinet.

Get ready with 2 plates and 2 knives.

Go to the cupboard and produce an ancient tin of corned beef.

Remove tin, preferably with a tin opener. Have a plaster ready for any potential injury.

Remove the corned beef and scrape off the dreadful white stuff around the edges, whatever it happens to be.

Place corned beef on board and cut into slices.

Stir in sprat oil for flavouring.

Spread the oiled slices uniformly onto Gaelic Bread.

You may use ordinary bread if you prefer but make sure you garnish with a sprinkling of heather to give that Scottish ambience.

You now have your very own pate that will fool the wisest guest.

Make up a story regarding its ingredients, using big words to substantiate your story.

Keep a straight face.

Serve professionally.

Covewae Escargots

Escargots is a posh word that found its way across The English Channel from France to settle in Great Britain. It's a foreign language word for snails.

Snails would never have been eaten had France never been invented but they are now a popular mouthful in restaurants around the world, but not on Covewae Island. We think outside the box, or should we say outside the shell. In passing, don't ever expect to find snails on the menu of a fast-food outlet.

On Covewae Island it refers to anything that lives in a shell, with the obvious exception of a giant turtle or a tortoise, two objects far too big to soak in oil and place on a dinnerplate. Regarding shells, do not be confused with overweight, unhealthy people in shell suits as they take even longer to cook and eat than turtles or tortoises. Smaller varieties of gastropods of various persuasions can be found in the rockpools around the island and make for a tasty starter that is certainly out of the ordinary.

With the normal escargot dish the plan is to remove whatever is inside with a pin maybe. Covewae Escargots are consumed in a different way.

Take a child's fishing net.

Scoop objects from the bottom of a rockpool and sift pebbles and stones, leaving just the small shells you are about to prepare.

Do not add salt as they've lived in the sea where there is plenty of salt.

Place the shells in your mouth in peanut fashion and munch furiously until you're certain that all the shells are emptied.

Remove shells from your mouth.

Think of a better starter to serve next time someone visits you and you may not suffer such a bad stomachache.

Do not throw the empty shells away as they can be spread onto discarded fishing line to make a handsome necklace, particularly if your meal is a birthday celebration. An ideal and cheap present if ever there was one.

Alternatively they can be shaken whilst listening to your party music after dinner.

Seaweed Soup

Seaweed Soup is a winner, a true winner. Before you attempt this starter in your own kitchen, do not get confused between seaweed with Swede. They sound similar but they are completely different. Seaweed lives in the water and Swedes live beside the water in Scandinavia. If you are still confused then seaweed cannot sing but Swedes can, so much so they won The Eurovision Song Contest.

Seaweed, in all its varieties, is a major source of iodine, amongst other medicinal gems, a healthy ingredient to assist thyroid issues.

Take a stroll along the coastline and find stranded bundles of seaweed. Give it a good shake to get rid of any unwanted residents who found it before you did and took up residence.

Place 1 litre of sea water in a saucepan to bring salt to the ingredients.

Place the saucepan on a bonfire and bring the sea water to the boil.

Throw the seaweed in the saucepan and stir the ingredients anti-clockwise in a vigorous fashion until it has a pulp consistency.

Do not add salt for the reasons already made obvious.

Add a few twigs as an alternative to floating parsley.

For those of you living near a freshwater lake why not try garnishing with a chopped lily-pad. It's a stupid idea and one that was given to us by someone who had a drink problem, so you try it at your peril.

Seagull Snack

Seagulls abound above Covewae Island and, boy, don't they let you know they're around. They are sacred creatures who are said to be ancient mariners who have returned from being lost at sea, which means all sailors of old must have had long, orange noses and angry temperaments.

It should be said there is actually no such bird as a seagull, as it's a general term for many different birds from gulls to terns. They are protected, not just by ample feathers, but from various laws that prevent them being hunted down like the poor pheasant.

Preparing a Seagull Snack is as simple as any food can be as a Seagull Snack is nothing more than a couple of stolen chips.

Dress in warm clothing and head for the sea.

Look to the sky where seagulls hover overhead as it means people are beneath them enjoying a pleasant snack of their own.

Keep your eye out for anyone eating in your vicinity.

Wave your arms around as a means of attracting the attention of squawking seagulls.

When anyone nearby looks up it is the moment to steal a chip.

Move away from the area, throw the chip on the ground and peck away at a speed of your choice.

Why not place the chip in your mouth and then throw it into the air for no reason whatsoever, the same as seagulls tend to do?

Be careful how you select your meal as seagulls also eat domestic waste and food from landfill sites so they are not great creatures to share your food with. They are omnivorous birds that also eat insects, so always be selective when preparing your Seagull Snack.

So there you have it, an unusual al-fresco style of dining, although it may be more suitable for eating alone than sharing a chip with a friend.

Mackerel Fin Soup

Mackerel Fin Soup is yet another delicacy unique to Covewae Island. It's the island's smaller alternative to Shark Fin Soup, a tasty soup not available on the island as they haven't seen a shark swimming offshore there for years, with or without fins. From a public health and safety aspect it's much safer to catch a mackerel than a shark anyway and it will allow much smaller soup bowls to be used. Catching a mackerel is nowhere as scary as enticing an angry shark into a rowing boat.

Capture seawater in a small saucepan, a pint or two, and boil slowly.

When the intention of cooking or boiling anything slowly it's better to use a controlled fire rather than a raging bonfire.

When the water has boiled add 25 mackerel fins. Stir the ingredients.

Mackerel fins are tiny, transparent things that don't have much taste. Because of this we suggest you add a tube of extra strong mints or a bar of chocolate at this stage of the preparation.

Add a sprig of parsley to taste.

Serve hot or cold, depending if your guests are late of if they arrive on time.

So there you have it, a wonderful selection of unique starters from Covewae Island. It's a delight to offer special delicacies that cannot be sampled anywhere else in the world.

Of course there are alternatives, most of which that we on the island perfectly understand.

Many diners choose not to order a starter, preferring to head straight for the main course. If you feel so inclined, have a late breakfast, around mid-afternoon, and make sure you're full before you begin your evening meal.

We now move towards the main course selection section and there is every chance you will find our offerings as unusual as the starters.

We are proud that all our meals consist of ingredients gathered around the island with very little if any items brought in from the mainland.

There is now work to be done as we prepare the main courses to satisfy your tastebuds. We would love to say you are in for a treat but we shall see.

If you wish to revert back to Shark Fin Soup as a more recognised alternative, we hope this poem will assist.

The trouble with Shark Fin Soup
Is the water must be very deep
Or else the shark can't swim around
So it will tend to go to sleep

For proper Shark Fin Soup
You should really see the fin
Going round and round the bowl
And then you are ready to begin

If the fin is underwater
It could be any soup at all
So always make sure the naughty shark
Doesn't roll up in a ball

Proper Shark Fin Soup
Will be special to your guests
But just in case they fall in
Give them all inflatable vests

Scottage Pie

Scottage Pie is the Covewae Island equivalent of the more acceptable Cottage Pie, yet far more distinctive. Instead of covering your ingredients with mashed potato, as is the norm, apply porridge instead. It can be served hot on a cold day or cold on a hot day, so always check the weather forecast before preparing this special meal.

Cook 500 grams of mince.

Add a sliced carrot.

Then slice an onion, but before you start to cry think about how the onion feels. Surely the onion is the one that should be crying as you end its life.

Stir the ingredients over the fire.

Remove from the flames.

Cover the ingredients with porridge.

If you wish to brown off the porridge like you would with mashed potato then sprinkle on brown sugar.

Return your dish to the fire and cook until you see or hear bubbling beneath the porridge.

Serve with a few peas or runner beans from vegetable patch.

If you have no vegetable patch serve with sliced stinging nettles.

Do not add brown sauce as it will ruin the taste.

Smoked Salmon

Smoked Salmon is a meal that everyone enjoys, apart from salmon who, quite rightly, aren't too keen. This is a rare offering as you will need to find a salmon that smokes, and very few partake in the filthy habit.

Smoked Salmon is a good source of protein, rich in Vitamin B12. It's particularly good for avoiding heart attacks, which makes you wonder why it isn't served by paramedics in the back of an ambulance.

Make you way to the water's edge where you see salmon leaping. These will be the fit and healthy salmon and not the smokers.

Wait for a salmon that cannot leap. Do not confuse a non-leaping salmon with a cod or any other fish covered in silvery scales.

Remove the cigarette from its mouth.

Fillet the fish removing all nicotine-stained fins.

If you live in Japan don't bother to cook the fish.

Smear Gaelic paste along the flesh.

Place the frying pan on your fire.

Cook fiercely for just 5 minutes.

Serve with sprinkled chives or sliced reed from the water's edge.

Hot Cross Buns

It can be argued that Hot Cross Buns are not exactly a main course, but, of course, that all depends how many Hot Cross Buns you intend to serve to each guest. Covewae Island is hardly the norm, a point proven by the preparation of this wholesome meal.

There was a time when Hot Cross Buns were only eaten during a Religious Festival but in more recent times they are now enjoyed all year around.

Make your home-made bread in the usual way.

Roll your home-made bread into rolls the size of cricket balls.

Place on a flat baking tray and heat on an open fire.

After 15 minutes turn the rolls over so the burnt crust is now on turn.

Using a sharp twig scratch a plus sign.

Take the removed crust and throw it to any circling seagull in the hope it goes away.

Do not serve more than 8 or 10 buns to your guest as this is excessive.

Potato Waffles

Waffles are usually served at breakfast but it's an evening tasty morsel on Covewae Island.

Dig up 4 potatoes and wash thoroughly whilst you ponder if new old potatoes are fresher than old new potatoes.

Sift 300 grams of flour into a bowl or a folded-up newspaper.

Add 4 eggs, hen's eggs and not ant's eggs. Remove the yolks and add the white of the eggs to the flour.

600ml of goat's milk.

Add 2 table spoonfuls of sea water as a salt substitute.

Stir with a strong piece of driftwood.

Follow a couple of bees around until you see where they live and steal a spoonful of honey.

Whilst enjoying your meal talk about anything that you know absolutely nothing about. Even if your guest falls asleep, don't stop waffling.

As we all know, waffles originated in America, the land of the free, and where some of our greatest wafflers reside or have done so in the past.

If you bore your guest so much they choose to go home then you have unexpectedly prepared tomorrow morning's breakfast.

Cooking Hints

So, beyond ensuring you do not confuse seaweed with a Swede, there are other clangers that may be waiting in hiding unless you are advised of their close proximity. Here are simple hints that may help.

Ignore the name, it's quite acceptable to stir coffee with a teaspoon.

Rhubarb is not the claw of a kangaroo, but a stalk that has poisonous leaves.

If your guest prefers their meat rare, then cook them something nobody has ever cooked before.

If someone asks you for a corkscrew they are not referring to an Irish prostitute.

If you are advised to cook something in a copper saucepan, break into the kitchen of a police station.

Never allow a team of chefs who have drunk too much lager to prepare you a meal. Remember, too many cooks soil the broth.

Warning! Never eat a meal in a casino as a seagull will steal your chips.

Nine Mints

This is the Covewae Island alternative to After Eight Mints, those delectable offerings at the end of any posh meal. Many will say that After Eight Mints cannot be beaten and that may well be the case, but Nine Mints is definitely another option and they're very easy to prepare.

Purchase a packet of extra strong mints next time you go shopping. It's difficult to make a mint of your own unless you have a brilliant business idea, so to save time and not bother about a three-year business plan, it's much easier to simply by a tube of things, ready-made.

Do not pay more than 35p or someone is making a mint on you.

Select a rather pretty bowl, or failing that, a flat piece of driftwood that's washed up on the beach.

Remove 9 mints from the packet.

Place in the bowl or on the wood.

Hand them to your guest.

Ensure your guest does not help themselves to 5 mints or they will have more than you.

Suck gently, do not risk biting into them if you have a loose tooth.

A delightful end to hopefully a delightful meal.

Cooking is fun and necessary too unless you choose to indulge in that Japanese raw stuff. Here are a few words to make it all even more fun.

Why do they put a sell-buy date on sour cream?

If you think an onion is the item of food that makes you cry, then rub a pineapple in someone's face and watch the tears flow.

How do you make an apple turnover? You start snoring and try to kick it out of bed.

What did one strawberry say to the raspberry? We seem to be in a jam.

Remember, if you don't like granulated sugar you can always lump it.

Why is there a 'best before' date on bottled spring water that's been underground for thousands of years?

Why isn't marmalade called orange jam?

Did you know The Earth's atmosphere is thinner than the skin of an apple and apple pips contain cyanide?

If that isn't scary enough, peanut oil is used to make nitro-glycerine, an explosive liquid used in the manufacture of dynamite.

Honey is the only food that doesn't go off, but if honey is so good for us all why don't bees live longer?

Did William Shakespeare call young pigs hamlets?

If a French cheese factory caught fire would there be nothing left but debrie?

Never tell an egg one of these jokes as it might crack up.

One more before we return to the menus, what's green and sings songs? Elvis Parsley.

Covewae Florentine

Eggs Benedictine is a popular breakfast in Europe, although it has never been as popular as porridge in Scotland where Covewae Island is situated.

Bake flat versions of Gaelic Bread by adding a sprinkling of heather.

Instead of the spinach used in Egg Florentine, substitute the spinach for seaweed.

Do not use bulbous dark-coloured seaweed for this offering. Search the coastline for a 'stringier' variety and shred to strands.

Warm the bread.

Place the cooked seaweed on the bread.

Bring seawater to the boil in a saucepan and add an egg for poaching. Hint. Add a spoonful of vinegar to the water to stop the white of the egg close to the yolk.

Place the poached egg on the seaweed.

Enjoy this breakfast treat.

Tofu Apples

Tofu, a favourite with vegetarians, is also known as bean curd. It's prepared by coagulating soy milk and pressing the resulting curds into blocks. As this substance can be moulded into various shapes here is an idea unique to Covewae Island, Tofu Apples.

Plant an apple tree, if you don't already have one in your garden, and wait for apples to appear. This may take a few years so be patient. Whilst waiting to pick the apples you will have time to walk the shoreline and gather small, straight twigs or other pieces of wood to act as sticks on which the apples will be placed when ready.

Remove the core of the apple.

Cover the apple in your especially prepared Covewae Tofu.

Place your piece of driftwood in the apple.

Warm gently by turning your apple, anti-clockwise, close to a bonfire, but not actually on it.

This luscious idea can be varied to suit your needs. If you want to produce a much smaller snack then substitute the apple for a grape. Conversely, if you want to completely pig out and think you can handle it, substitute the apple for a watermelon. The choice is yours.

Bakewell Tartan

As Covewae Island is situated somewhere in The Atlantic Ocean off the Scottish mainland, it is only right to include a tartan in the ingredients of one of our most peculiar delights.

Tartan originated as a coloured woven wool, as horizontal and vertical twines, to make various varieties for various clans. Where such coloured sheep that provide the wool can be found remains a mystery in a similar way to The Loch Ness Monster.

Bakewell Tart originates from the English town of Bakewell in Derbyshire and we are proud to offer our Covewae Island variation.

Remove a sponge from the sea.

Chop a few almonds into lots of tiny fragments and sprinkle the result into the sponge.

Warm the sponge on your open fire until it is baked well.

Whilst still warm, wrap the sponge in a tartan scarf and let it stand for a few minutes.

Remove tartan scarf.

Sea sponges are very difficult to cut into slices so it's best to just tuck into the whole thing. Take a few bites and then pass around what is left.

Own model bears no resemblance whatsoever to an original Bakewell Tart, but we make no excuses, as our version, wrapped in a scarf, is easier to transport around and eat as and whenever the mood takes your fancy.

Seahorse Radish Sauce

Horseradish is a popular dollop to have on the side of your plate and we are delighted to reveal the secret ingredients of our very own sauce.

The original horseradish is used to traditionally add taste to roast beef, but we do not eat roast beef on Covewae Island, so much so we don't even have a clue what beefs look like, let alone cook the things.

Wade into the sea and keep your eyes peeled.
Find a pack of seahorses and round them up, using a lasso if necessary.
Place half a dozen of the captured seahorses into a bowl, removing any saddles or jockeys.
Take a dozen radishes and crush them into a pulp.
Mix the seahorses with the radish paste, stirring rigorously.
Place on the side of a plate and try to come up with some kind of meal that would benefit from such a sauce. In case you struggle with its use the upside is Seahorse Radish Sauce has a long shelf-life.

Rock Cakes

Any island, such as Covewae, considers Rock Cakes as an essential and yet easy to prepare snack. It's hardly surprising when considering the number of rocks that can be gathered on a small island. To prove the point, if you ever walk the length of The Sahara Desert you will never find a shop that sells Rock Cakes due to their scarcity.

The simple question is how on earth can you make rocks a tasty offering? Can it be done? The answer is yes, as you will find sticks of rock available at seaside resorts all around Great Britain.

It's not uncommon to eat rock along with home-made bread on Covewae Island. We call it rock and roll.

Food for two.

Make a pint of custard.

Find 2 rocks about the size of tennis balls and wash them thoroughly to eradicate the taste of salt.

Place in a bowl and cover with the custard.

Use an arched piece of driftwood to scoop up the custard.

When all the custard has been consumed throw the rock back into the sea and accept the idea of eating Rock Cakes as the most ridiculous of all suggestions, even on Covewae Island.

Hey, you gave it a go, but the time has now come to try something not quite so damaging to your teeth.

There are numerous very simple ideas and thoughts that don't need their own pages of explanation. Here are some examples.

Dundee Cake, take a train to Dundee and buy a cake when you get there.

Nan Bread, a necessity with any curry but quite simply bread made by your grandmother.

Twiglets. Our own version by gathering twigs on a windy day and smothering them in Marmite. We love Marmite on Covewae, just saying.

Jellyfish and ice-cream, perfect for children's' parties.

Never serve bread and butter pudding with a slice of bread and butter as it's pointless.

What would happen if you put instant coffee in a microwave?

What do you get for a Covewae dolphin that sings out of tune? A piano tuna.

Are pork chops slang for the mouths of pigs?

Just in passing, what's the difference between salt and table salt? No idea.

What would a banana slip on?

How did a lovely bunch of coconuts stand in a row when coconuts don't have legs?

An equal weight of potatoes are two hundred times cheaper than chips.

You can never buy a curry, you only rent it for a couple of hours.

Are blackberry and apple pies filled with mobile phones and if so why isn't an orange included? Back to the menu.

Covewae Shepherd's Pie

Shepherd's Pie and Cottage Pie are very similar in appearance so you need to look very closely. That's not the case on Covewae Island. A Covewae Shepherd's Pie is covered in hair as opposed to only mashed potato and a Covewae Cottage Pie contains the same filling but its topping is thatched with twigs from the forest area of the island.

Dinner for two.

Light the bonfire.

Remove the jackets from 4 potatoes.

By removing their jackets they will be cold so they will need warming up.

Boil the potatoes by placing a saucepan on the bonfire.

Overcook the spuds so they are easier to mash.

To mash the potatoes use a strong stick, preferably with holes in.

Fill a dish with seaweed, tomatoes and a sliced onion, as if you were preparing Covewae Spaghetti Bolognese.

Spread the mashed potato across the top of the ingredients.

Add a shepherd's hair, unless you have a bald shepherd to hand, in which case drape a bobble hat across the top of the dish.

Finally, scrape the top layer off as a complete and unhealthy waste of time and serve the remaining contents.

Please note that the remaining contents are the same as Spaghetti Bolognese and Lasagne, so you have a choice as to what you wish to call your dish and what to tell you guests.

If you happen to be dining with a shepherd just remember it's his pie and not yours.

If you require a more sensible recipe for the same meal, we hope this poem will assist. It isn't how we cook on Covewae Island but I may be a more sensible alternative.

Finding a lonely shepherd sitting on a hill
The next part of this recipe will require some skill
Without him knowing anything, slice off an arm and leg
If he spots what you are doing just ignore his beg

If it's a large dinner party and large numbers you have got
Don't mess about with arms and legs it's best to cook the lot
Lay him in a dish and the rest I'm sure you know
Cover in potato from his head down to his toe

Sprinkle him with onions and a spice or two to taste
If he has a beer gut add more pastry around his waist
Put him in the oven for a quarter of an hour

If he isn't crispy try turning up the power

His plan will be to get out
So there is every chance he will try
But just keep him where he is
Because you've made a Shepherd's Pie.

Pea Nuts

We all know peanuts are full of protein. It's a fact that over one third of the peanuts eaten in the whole world are consumed by the Chinese population.

That may seem quite a sweeping statement of fact until we compare the population of China with other smaller countries. There's every chance that those nice Chinese people eat one third of just about everything produced and peanuts are obviously no exception. At least the rest of the world is left with two-thirds.

So let us introduce you to a new kind of peanut that the Chinese have no interest in whatsoever because they probably don't know much about what it is. Covewae Island has never welcomed a Chinese tourist to its shores, mainly because there are no direct flights from Tokyo or London Heathrow. The clue, regarding the difference between original peanuts and Pea Nuts, lies within the fact that our unique dish is two words and not just one.

Scrape a selection of small shells from the beach, the smaller the more suitable.
Empty whatever exists inside the shells.
Pick a handful of peas from your vegetable patch or a tin of peas from a supermarket if you don't happen to have a vegetable patch.

Place one pea in each shell.

Place them in a small bowl ready to serve.

It's said that traces of men's urine can be found in a pub's bowl of peanuts, but that's nothing compared with the seagull poo that we have to contend with.

Enjoy the protein.

Tea Cakes

One of our favourite afternoon delights on Covewae Island. It's always a pleasure to sit in the garden, looking out on The Atlantic Ocean, enjoying tea and Tea Cakes whilst watching the seals at play in the natural pool they have made their home. Actually, at play is hardly a term to use when describing seals because of them look downright miserable apart from Andrew and Wilder, a couple who have been good friends of us all.

Not having a bakery on the island it's yet another case of improvising and making this recipe very much our own with our limited resources.

Fill a saucepan with I litre of sea water.

Collect the used teabags that have been stored away and place half a dozen in the saucepan.

Bring the contents to the boil, stirring rigorously.

Meanwhile, make a pastry mix of flour and water and mould into small cup-like shapes.

Allow the water and teabags to cool and when appropriate fill each pastry with the mix.

Cover the mix completely with the pastry and place on the fire until the pastry has developed into a nice, crusty consistency.

Allow to cool once again.

Watch out for seagulls overhead as this is one of their favourite foods to attack from on high.

Herring In The Hole

Toad In The Hole is a British speciality that no-one else anywhere in the world finds at all succulent. It's hardly surprising as the very name is enough to ruin anyone's appetite.

The major problem we have with this offering is that no toads live on Covewae Island and if they did we wouldn't cook them anyway, even if we did find them living in holes. So we needed to come up with an alternative, one of our most difficult culinary exercises, thus our very own Herring In The Hole.

After extensive research we discovered that traditional Toad In The Hole is nothing more than sausages loitering in Yorkshire pudding.

Catch 4 herring by using a size 10 hook bedecked with a tiny strip of mackerel or even a strip of silver paper.

Fillet the fish by simply removing the backbone, head and tail.

Throw the unwanted parts to the seagulls as a decoy to keep them away from the main ingredients.

Concoct a mixture of flour, eggs and goats' milk, stirring until a smooth mixture before placing in a flat pan ready for action.

Place the herring in the mixture and cook on an established bonfire until the mixture has risen in the hope of escaping the flames.

You now have a delightful meal that both yourself, your guest and all surviving toads will enjoy.

Covewae Casserole

A warming winter dish that allows you to use up various vegetables you have grown but have left to go a tad limp. In a casserole nobody will notice their sad appearance as they all swim around together in a most colourful myriad of nutritious delight.

The fact is that anything can be slung into a casserole so it's more a rubbish bin or a local tip more than a meal. You can use old vegetables, fish, other items of seafood that you find lifeless on the shore, even pencil sharpener shavings and old magazine pages if you so wish, no-one will know. So, basically, it's your chance to be creative and imaginative.

Take the largest saucepan you have and give it good clean if you've previously used it as a bucket when cleaning your windows.

Throw in everything you can think of because that's what the French did back in the 19th Century when they came up with the idea. We leave the ingredients entirely up to you.

The beauty of the Covewae Casserole is that it can be cooked over a long period of time, possibly years knowing the French, so you have time to do other things, for example, see how many words you can make from the letters contained in the word casserole, not using any letter twice. There are 74, thus giving you enough time to let your meal simmer and be ready for your consumption.

Serve in bowls and place a few blades of wild grass on top to add a little more colour.

Covewae Stroganoff

Covewae Stroganoff is a similar dish to the aforementioned Covewae Casserole, but with a few extra ingredients. Words don't come much stranger than Stroganoff so it's interesting to know how the name came about.

It was all down to a certain chef who worked for a wealthy Russian family in St Petersburg and by all accounts he entered a cooking contest in 1891, which he won. He named his gold-prize dish after his boss Count Ravel Alexandrovich Stroganov and the rest as they say is geography, so long as you don't change the subject.

Of course it would have been much easier all round if his employer's name had been Smith, Jones or Brown, but such surnames are rare in Russia so there was little likelihood that it would come to be.

With such a history we just had to name our own example of the meal as Covewae Casserole, not having any Russian landowner on the island to be honoured with such a dedication. That's the history, and now for the dish itself.

Use the same weary ingredients as those in the Covewae Casserole on the previous page.

Place a carton of milk in the Sun until it looks a little on the lumpy side.

Chop a dozen mushrooms and add to the mix.

Finally, add the white of an egg.

Stir gently whilst cooking upon the fading embers of a spent bonfire.

Serve with Gaelic Bread.

Covewae Rarebit

It's well acknowledged that Welsh Rarebit was thrown together in Wales by Welsh chefs. That doesn't mean our island couldn't come up with its own version. There are no copyright restrictions on food recipes.

We are talking of nothing more than cheese on toast, disguised by a word only known to the Welsh, rarebit. Being a Welsh word it's surprising it doesn't start with a double L as most of their other words seem to do, but in this case they forgot. So, how to prepare cheese on toast.

Bake a home-made loaf on the bonfire.

Cut into edible slices, allowing the meal to be eaten with a knife and fork or with the fingers.

Cheese must be added while the bread is still warm to allow the underneath part of the cheese to melt.

Cut your favourite cheese into slices and place them on the bread and place the whole thing back onto the bonfire.

When the cheese starts to bubble, probably due to being in pain, your meal is ready.

Spread Covewae Chutney, described on the next page, across the top.

Serve with pride.

Do not confuse the above with plain old cheese on toast or a cheese sandwich that has been sun-bathing and got itself a bit on the warm side.

Stuart's Chutney

If you have read the story of The Covewae Kid you will know that Stuart is the local police officer who fends off crime in the area by riding around on his pushbike at great haste. In all honesty, he doesn't have too much to do during his working hours, his last legal action being booking a chicken for speeding. It never reached court and the chicken was let off with a warning. So here are the ingredients if you wish to emulate his highly acclaimed invention.

Purchase a bottle of malt pickling vinegar and empty the contents into a saucepan.

Pick apples from a tree, even if you don't the tree. Think back your schooldays of scrumping.

Peel the apples and chop them into small pieces.

Add brown sugar.

If you don't have brown sugar then use ordinary sugar and add some rotting leaves. It will soon turn brown.

Slice 4 onions into small pieces and add to mix.

If you find any currents you'd forgotten you had in your food cupboard add them too.

Add a few twigs to give that earthy taste.

Bring all to the boil on the bonfire.

When all is bubbling, remove them from the bonfire and leave the saucepan on the side of the fire to simmer gently for 45 minutes.

Place the content in jars and use whenever you deem suitable, particularly ideal for late suppers beneath the Moon.

Duckweed Pate

Yet another pate recipe unique to the kitchen at Covewae Island. It seems that various pate producers add their own ingredients so why shouldn't Covewae? Others offer flavours such as salmon, pheasant and other unfortunate creatures, but none throw in bits of driftwood and creepy-crawlies from the beach.

To copy this suggestion you need to find an area of fairly stagnant water where duckweed thrives. Scrape the weed from the surface of the water and you're in business. If you see any creatures hanging around whilst you harvest your weed do not be confused between the common duck and the duckweed platypus, a rare creature in Scotland, but not as rare as The Loch Ness Monster.

Take a stroll along a beach.

Gather the duckweed, strain the water and chop into small pieces.

Open a tin of luncheon meat and do the same again, chopping away until almost a paste.

Mix the duckweed and luncheon meat.

Chop 2 onions and add.

Add 2 tablespoonfuls of seawater just to make sure you will feel slightly ill.

Spread the pate onto Gaelic Bread.

Serve without telling your guests of your bizarre ingredients.

Covewae Salad

The first words of advice we give when you prepare Covewae Salad is to not overcook and burn the ingredients, advice for those who have never prepared a salad before and maybe don't even know what it is.

The beauty of a salad is that you can basically get away with blue murder and sling anything you like in a bowl so long as it's cold and a colour that resembles something natural to nature.

Here on Covewae Island we take great pride in discovering ingredients to make our salads unique. We use items washed up on the seashore, the strangest has to be a message in a bottle that may well have come from a galleon of many years ago. The enthralling message reduced us on the island to tears. Written in Olde English script it is translated as thus.

'To whom it may concern. I'm so happy you have found this bottle washed up on your beach, especially if It has arrived on a Thursday. I write to say never include this bottle or the message within a salad, this Is a bottle not a salad or a bunch of radishes, and it has probably passed its sell-by date and may cause tummy ache. God Save The King.'

We took his advice but there are other washed up items mentioned in these pages that may just work. If not, rip the page out this book and read on.

Maybe a few more funny lines would help you digest our content with more safety and satisfaction.

What can you do to help a dying fish? Fit a plaice-maker.

What's the easiest food to prepare if you are in a hurry? A Pizza Cake.

What do you cook if an old member of Parliament and a famous songwriter come to dinner? Curry and Rice.

What's the best food found on Covewae Island that will calm you down? A marshmellow.

What can you do to rose bush suffering from constipation? Pruning.

What do you call the first fish that helped with the menus in this book? A flounder member.

Remember, not all sharks are car dealers.

What do you call a line of people waiting to buy a doll in a toyshop? A Barbie queue.

Here's an interesting fact, did you know a shrimp's heart is in its tongue?

If you order a chicken and an egg online which will come first?

We saw a hen on Covewae Island staring at a lettuce and slices of cucumber. It was a case of chicken sees a salad.

A little boy walks into a fishmonger and asks the shopkeeper 'Mummy said can she have a kilogram of whale-meat and can you put the head in for the cat?'

A friend of mine has a vegetable patch. It's on his arm and stops his craving for vegetables.

Never put vinegar in your ear as you'll end up with pickled hearing.

Grilled Grey Mullet

Grey mullet are friendly fish that hang out in the shallows around Covewae. They're also very shy and don't seem to be answer to any question they may be grilled on. For that reason they live in perfect harmony with us and are safe from harm.

Because of this mutual appreciation society we do not feature any mullet within our menus, so why the heading for this page? We digress to describe one of our inhabitants as a kind of diversion.

Hamish McDonald was the one-time owner of Covewae Island, as explained in the book, The Covewae Kid. After living here for many years he left the island to live with a dental nurse, as you shall read in more depth in that book. Here is his description, the menu of his appearance.

An old, weathered man.
Large staring eyes with a yellow, jaundiced hint, just like a fish.
His hair is grey, short at the sides and sadly too long at the back. The style he created, because of his association with Covewae Island, is now known as a mullet. In the case of this ageing man, his own hairstyle can be described as a grey mullet.
You will often see older men, trying to hold onto their youth as they walk along the street, who admire

Hamish McDonald, even if you have never heard of him yourself.

Breast of Shrimp

A remarkable dish unique to Covewae Island, never seen anywhere else in the world as no chef living anywhere else can be bothered to attempt it due to the tedious work involved. Let us begin by describing the lowly shrimp in intricate detail to ascertain its nutritional value and why it is such a delicious roast dinner. It all makes difference for the more usual chicken, pork or roast beef alternatives.

The shrimp is a shellfish creature, quite misleading as it is happy to share its assets with other shrimps. They have ten legs upon which they travel the seabed, with a head that goes halfway down the length of its body. The rest, from the end of the head to the tail, is actually the abdomen, the edible part its body which we call the breast on this particular dish.

Catch 100 shrimps from a rockpool in a child's net.

This may take a long time so take a flask of coffee and sandwiches with you on your journey to the water's edge.

Remove the heads and tails, known as tossing, and remove each soft shell.

You now have 100 tiny breasts that when boiled in water provide the main structure of a delectable meaty dish.

Once lightly boiled, place the breasts in a roasting tray and sprinkle with 3 teaspoons of vegetable oil.

Like all roast dinners, add roast potatoes and Brussel sprouts.

Undressed Crab

The shrimp, mentioned on the previous page, is a member of the much sought-after crab family. Crab is available in most coastal restaurants, expensive as it is. The big problem for a chef is that crabs are heavily protected, probably the reason they live longer than prawns.

It's a strange play on words of the English language as a dressed crab actually describes a crab that has been undressed. On the island we use as much of the crabmeat as is possible and even the leftovers are slung into a saucepan to produce crab soup, something that never seems to appear in tins on supermarket shelves, with the exception of France where crab bisque soup is sold. So how do we undress a crab?

This is how crab becomes part of a crushed nation.

Remove their pair of claws, the most favourite part of the crab.

Beneath the shell is a tail that is seldom seen.

Claws and tail are removed by twisting and not pulling.

Crab is always served traditionally with brown bread.

On the island we serve with brown Gaelic Bread, which is achieved by following direction on a previous page to produce our unique bread, but as you bake over the bonfire cover the bread in rotting leaves or twigs that have fallen from trees. This will ensure your bread is brown as expected.

Allow the crabmeat to cool.

Pick an apple from a tree and slice it in two.

Cover the crabmeat in apple juice.

It's the accepted thing to use lemon juice but we have no lemon trees on the island and apple juice makes a wonderful substitute.

Place a side-salad on the plate made from seaweed strands.

Serve as a special dish to someone who you don't really regard as special.

Sardines In Sauce

Sardines, also known as pilchards, are easily found in the sea. There are literally millions of the things swimming around. Despite their relatively small size, a little over 6 inches, they can live for up to 13 years, far longer than so many other fish of greater size. They are a chef's delight because they can be eaten whole, the sardines not the chef, and therefore kitchen preparation is minimal.

Sardines swim in huge shoals so they're not too difficult to catch. The chances are if you catch one you'll end of up with thousands of the things, so they are a suitable menu for large wedding receptions or other parties. No such things happen on Covewae so it gives the opportunity to return many of your captured fish back into the ocean.

Sardines have their own oil which assists the cooking over an open fire, so, yes, cooking is easy.

Spread 6 sardines in a line.
Light the bonfire.
Turn the fish after just 5 minutes.
Serve on Gaelic Bread.
Do not add salt as they've lived in the sea for over a decade so the hint of salt will be there.

Peppered Sardines

Sardines, not requiring much classy preparation, can be eaten in various ways, all of them simple. Peppered Sardines has to be the simplest and therefore the shortest in this collection. It isn't the slightest bit funny for the sardine but this recipe is guaranteed to make you smile.

Take sardines out your freezer
Wrap them up because they'll be freezing
Then cover them with pepper
Until they all start sneezing
You know exactly what every sneeze means
You have had a success with Peppered Sardines

Apple and Blackberry Pie

Here is a chance to get rid of your old mobile phones. Nearly every bedside cabinet has one or two of the redundant machines lying dormant and unwanted. Here is the solution that may not be particularly mouth-watering but good for environment, so well worth a go.

Apple and Blackberry Pie is a good old traditional pudding and therefore nothing special, except that a Covewae chef has come up with the idea of adding an orange, an original addition and an assurance that no phones would be left out when emptying the bedside cabinet.

Line your old mobile phones on a baking tray.
Remove all batteries as they will make the taste too acidic.
Cover them in pastry.
Do not cook a mobile phone still in use as the pastry will affect reception, especially if it soaks into the microphone.
Cook on an open fire until the horrible smell disappears.
The ingredients will be hard to chew so do not serve to friends with dentures. Yes, mobile phones are a filling that can damage a filling.
If your guest is late why not give them a call with your new pudding? Of course not, the phones are dead,

that would be ridiculous, and one thing about this book is that it certainly isn't ridiculous.

Corn On The Cod

A wonderful imaginative recipe that has nearly won many awards, but not quite. If you are thinking of corn on the cob then you are way off radar. This is different and will be easier to hold.

Hire a boat.

Set up your tackle, using a size 8 hook on 15lb breaking strain line.

Use mackerel strip as bait, as usual.

Catch a cod.

Fillet the fish.

You will find cod have big heads out of proportion with the rest of their bodies, so it's easy to work out the fleshy edible part as it's wedged between the big head and the tail, which is at the back of the fish just in case you've never seen a cod swimming around as opposed to sitting in a warm cabinet in a fish and chip shop.

T Bone Skate

We would love to offer T Bone Skate as one of the delicacies on our Covewae Island menu, but unfortunately this is nothing more than a typing error that wasn't picked up on the proof-read. No restaurant can offer a T Bone Skate to its customers purely because of the huge size of a skate.

The skate is a member of the Ray community and they are giant flatfish that look like kites. Think back to when you constructed a kite when you were a child and you will recall the wooden stick structure, a like a cross, that held the thing together. It's a similar construction that holds a skate together, and there isn't a plate in Europe big enough to accommodate such a meal, let alone us on Covewae Island.

A skate and its fine qualities will be mentioned elsewhere within these pages so all is not lost if you wish to sample its taste, but a T Bone Skate just happens to be out of the question, thus making this particular page a complete and utter waste of time, not dissimilar pages here that also seem to be a complete and utter waste of time too.

It's time to turn the page and return to a far more sensible suggestion.

Angel Fish Delight

A scrumptious sweet for people of all ages and one that comes in so many beautiful colours. The only problem here is that angel fish don't live anywhere near Covewae Island, unless an islander happens to own an aquarium. This may well be the dawning of the age of aquariums. But don't let that put you off as it's well worth the extra effort to enjoy such a splendid dish. Each angel fish is blessed of between 5 and 8 stripes that fade as they age, just like us.

Angel fish come from The Amazon, and that doesn't mean they arrive by post in a box, but the fact they come from The Amazon Basin itself. Their strange shape and colourings allow them to hide among underwater roots and plants, so if you intend to serve them as a meal make sure they aren't wrapped in seaweed or your guests won't know they're sitting on a nice slice of Gaelic Bread.

Fry them for no more than 30 seconds before placing them on the bread.

They are basically the highwaymen of the ocean, prying on smaller fish with an element of surprise.

Stuart's Pickled Onions

Stuart, the local copper who patrols Covewae Island is proud of his chutney and pickled onions, probably prepared in a copper saucepan. We are delighted to expose one of his greatest secrets, how his delectable, pickled onions stand out from the pickled crowd.

Stuart takes an onion on the town
You know what he must be thinking
To get an onion truly pickled
He has to make sure they're all drinking

He gives it tots of vodka
Followed by tots of gin
He soaks them in vinegar when they get home
That's what gives them brown skin

That's how Stuart makes them
Pickled onions to give to friends
Now you know his secret
That's where this poem ends

Wood Pigeon Pie

Pigeons are considered a real nuisance by many people, with the exception of course of those who race them and make a fortune in prize money. On Covewae Island we welcome them with open arms to our shores as they don't get on with seagulls too well, who does? Similar to The Battle of Britain, over our heads, they fight for aerial supremacy and many is the time when pigeons see off the wicked seagulls. For that we give thanks and lest we never forget they flew on the front line as messengers during The First and Second World Wars. How can we possibly cook creatures that have won medals for bravery?

Because of this aerial contribution, we islanders repay the birds by not adding them to any menu and thus play their part in keeping them safe from harm. It doesn't stop them dropping on us what pigeons seem to enjoy dropping on us, and their constant cooing is an annoyance, but at least they don't swoop down and steal our chips like those naughty seagulls. You may not think so but they are on our side, and you must never cook friends for other friends.

When we cook a Covewae pigeon pie
We know it's for the good
Especially for the poor pigeon
If we only cook ones made of wood

Pigeons don't like being cooked
It makes them feel far too hot
But it goes of course without saying
A wood pigeon definitely does not

That's why we prepare a Wood Pigeon Pie
It really cannot be beat
Just make sure you spit out the splinters
As our speciality you eat

Sponges

Sponges are mouth-watering treats for everyone and being an island there is an abundance of sponges all around Covewae, albeit all of them being underwater and brightly coloured. Their closeness to us allows us to invent uses for them that make Covewae Island unique.

Unlike a Victoria sponge, a chocolate sponge or a finger sponge, our Covewae sponges are not for consumption. Instead, they are used as an aid to hygiene and therefore they should feature as part of every menu we offer to you on these pages. We recommend you include a sponge with your own preparations, just don't try eating them.

So as you prepare in your kitchen remember to wash your hands before you handle any ingredients, They presumably serve the same function in the ocean, laying on the seabed and keeping the water clean, therefore playing a major part in the preservation of the environment.

Prawn Wellington

This is obviously an alternative to the popular Beef Wellington.

Find an old Wellington boot you no longer wear.

Take it from the utility room to the kitchen and scrape off age-old mud.

Remove any socks that have taken root.

Pour 1 pint of seawater into the boot.

Add two handfuls of freshly ambushed prawns.

Add chopped mushrooms but never use toadstools unless you have invited someone to dinner who you really don't like and would be pleased to see the back of them.

Stir the ingredients slowly over the embers of a bonfire. Do not apply extreme heat as the Wellington will be made of rubber and the smell will be disgusting as it melts.

Serve with roast potatoes and chopped cabbage from your vegetable patch. If you don't have a vegetable patch then try and find a tin of cabbage. You'll be lucky.

If need be substitute the cabbage for peas, those little green things that definitely do come in tins.

All we are saying, is give peas a chance.

It may be of interest to discover how the original Beef Wellington came to be as The Duke of Wellington is mentioned in The Covewae Kid book. Of course, it may not be of any interest whatsoever but here it is anyway.

Beef Wellington

Every second day of May
To The Duke of Wellington we must say
Well done Nosey at Waterloo
You taught that chap a thing or two

We must also praise him for being shrewd
When it came to hanging on to food
On the battlefield there was nothing harder
As they had no cans or well-stocked larder

That's when Wellington was astute
He stored some beef inside his boot
Oh how The Duke of Wellington cursed
As he forgot to take his foot out first

Whilst Nelson guided the British navy
Wellington walked with his foot in gravy
Slopping around first left then right
He must have looked a proper sight

Despite the ridicule and the scorn
Beef Wellington on that day was born
All you need is a lump of beef
It it's wrapped undo it with your teeth

A Wellington boot you must add

Size 8, well that's what Wellington had
Into the oven gas mark 9
Thirty minutes should do fine

Your meal will sadly smell like rubber
And even worse will taste of blubber
To round it off chew a pickled onion
Poor Wellington had to nibble on a bunion

So maybe our alternative isn't so bad
When you think of the dinner Wellington had
Covewae Wellington he would have chosen
And his feet would have not been frozen

Turbot Dabs

This can be described as nothing less than a flatfish delight. If the title of this speciality has brought sherbet dabs to your mind then you about to be bitterly disappointed. The only similarity is both things happen to come on a stick as one is confectionary for children and the other is a kind of kebab.

Find a straight thin item of driftwood from the beach and scrape clean with a gloved hand.

Catch a turbot.

Catch 3 to 4 dabs as they are much smaller than turbot.

Cut each fish into small pieces.

Slice 2 tomatoes.

Place them alternately onto the piece of driftwood.

Do not use a bonfire to cook this speciality.

Light a small fire, preferably outdoors so as not to char your carpet.

Turn slowly for 4 minutes or until you get bored and your arm aches.

Serve the meal on the driftwood with a salad side dish.

Mushroom Soup

A Covewae Island favourite on cold, winter days, but be warned, preparation can take an eternity. Before deciding on this offering please ensure you recognise the difference between a mushroom and a toadstool. This method of preparing our own version of Mushroom Soup has been described as pure poetry, and here is the reason why.

Mushroom Soup is very tasty
It needs patience so don't be hasty
First you find a discarded bin
And fill it with compost to the brim

Add some water to a level high
Or else the soup will be too dry
Then you lift the aforementioned bin
And find a cupboard to place it in

In about six months if all goes well
The first you'll notice is a pungent smell
In seven months round the table group
You've Just created Mushroom Soup

And so you see, this isn't an ideal meal for guests who turn up, uninvited, at the last minute. But hey, if they turn up at the last minute what do they expect? Give them a cup of tea and a biscuit.

Interesting Food Facts

As a slight diversion, here are some facts you may find of interest. They will certainly give you food for thought.

It's a fact that chocolate used to be used as money for wheeling and dealing. Cocoa beans used to be counted the same way as coins by The Aztec tribes.

We all know the nutritious value of honey but it's actually a mix of nectar and bee puke. By the way, bees need to visit over a million flowers to make just one pound of honey. That's 5,000 flowers for each spoonful.

All polar bears are left-handed, something to remember when laying out the cutlery if you've invited one to dinner.

It takes a lobster seven years to grow to just one pound in weight.

A cucumber is 96% water and yet it contains enough electrolytes to cure a violent hangover. Just think about that, it's only 4% less than The Atlantic Ocean that surrounds Covewae Island.

You may have noticed if you place lemons and limes in a drink the lemons will float and limes will sink.

It proves Archimedes was right because it's all down to density and tiny air-holes in a lemon.

Almonds are the seeds of flowers and not nuts.

Up to Victorian times, people washed their hair with a mixture of water and beetroot as a means of preventing dandruff. That's why some gardeners can look marooned on an island such as ours.

Egg yolks are the most proficient way of absorbing Vitamin D, the best defence to a threatening virus. Good to know since the 2020 enemy arrived.

This isn't an old wife's tale. If you run hot water when slicing an onion it will stop you crying, until the bills roll in.

The expiry date on bottled water is actually not for the water itself but more for the bottle it is in. Water doesn't have proteins or sugars which means that it won't "go off" in the way that food does. However, if left open to air, it's chemical composition will change as it absorbs carbon dioxide.

There's every chance a raw oyster will still be alive when you eat it, which gives a different meaning to eating something to make your stomach move.

Clam Chops

We don't eat much meat on Covewae Island due to a distinct lack of animals that aren't friendly pets we have come attached to. So, instead of Lamb Chops, why not give our special Clam Chops a try?

Clams are small shellfish that play a major role in the environment balance as they do their best to clean the ocean. Razor clams are a great choice because once you have eaten them you can have a shave with the shell.

Take a netful of clams and wash thoroughly.
Unlike lamb there is no fat around the edges so they're ready for consumption.
Cook over an open fire.
Add mint to taste.
Peel potatoes and bring them to the boil.
Serve with boiled potatoes and greens.
Clams are a great alternative to oysters to serve to a guest you don't really fancy because although oysters are aphrodisiac clams most certainly aren't and their smell avoids kissing at the table.

Clams in brine are a true delicacy and it can be made by shelling the clams and leaving them in a jar of sea water.

Fish Thumbs

Why hasn't any chef come up with this idea before? We all know fish fingers are a delight for little ones, so why not have Fish Thumbs for adults?

Bake a loaf of Gaelic Bread and then attack it with a cheese-grater until there are enough crumbs to cover a decent sized herring.

Catch the herring and fillet.

Roll the herring in the breadcrumbs, adding the white of an egg to stop the breadcrumbs falling off and making a mess on the floor.

If the white of an egg isn't to hand then have brush and dustpan ready or you will be invaded by mice.

Cook lightly for 5 to 6 minutes, the herring not the mice.

Serve with chips and peas.

If serving this dish to children please be aware you can use any fish as they will cover the meal with gallons of tomato ketchup, known as Tommy K, so they will have no idea what they're eating anyway.

Serve with confidence.

Hot Dogfish

We found a similar recipe in The United States of America, but this variety is well and truly a Covewae Island invention.

Back in the days of your grandparents, dogfish was served up in the local fish and chip shop under the name of Rock Salmon. Dogfish are nothing to do with the salmon family, in fact they're not even on speaking terms, but the idea was the new name would make the fish more enticing to customers who were fed up with cod.

Dogfish are little shark-looking beasts that swim around near the coastline and can be caught on just about anything as they are complete scavengers. Be warned, their skin is as sharp as sandpaper if you run your hand the wrong way down its back. The benefit of this is that once you have skinned the fish you can give your kitchen table a going over with the skin and remove annoying coffee mug marks.

Catch a dogfish and skin with care. Use a size 6 hook and use an old sick as bait as they eat anything.

Place the fish on the bonfire for just 3 minutes. In case you don't have a timer, boil an egg at the same time and the fish will be ready the same time as the egg.

Serve with chips and peas, nothing too grand.

Ideal for a guest who isn't worthy of any effort.

The only dilemma is trying to determine the difference between a dogfish and a catfish.

Dogfish love chasing catfish
That's a fun thing for that fish
Unless the catfish is big
And if dogfish doesn't twig
It may well end up as a flatfish

Hop Scotch Eggs

Hop Scotch Eggs is a wonderful ingredient for party gatherings, particularly if your guests are boring and you need to stay awake. Quite simply it's nothing more than eating a boiled egg, covered in breadcrumbs, whilst hopping around on one leg. It's a particularly fun meal after drinking copious amount of home-made wine or cider.

Dig up a piece of white chalk and draw squares, numbered 1 to 10, on your carpet.

Do you remember at school the teacher used chalks of various colours? Where did that come from? We have chalk in the ground on Covewae Island but it isn't multi-coloured.

Boil seawater in a saucepan

Boil 6 eggs, longer than is recommended to make sure they the yolks are hard.

Cover the eggs with Gaelic breadcrumbs.

Stand on one leg on square one for no real reason.

Take one bite of the egg before moving onto square 2, and so on.

By the time you reach square 10 you will be feeling sick so stop hopping and have a lie down.

Tossing The Conger

Speaking of party games, here is another. This isn't a meal in any way whatsoever but it's good fun at a meal and its derivation is from the Scottish Highland Games event of tossing the caber. Big, bearded warriors pick up a tree and try to throw it a few feet whilst grunting.

Tossing the Conger is a similar game. To play along you must wear a white vest and a kilt or you will be disqualified.

Hire a rowing boat and head your guests out to sea where an old wreck has been sleeping for over a century.

Place a mackerel strip on a hook and wait for your fishing rod to buckle.

Once you hook a conger eel the fun really begins.

Congers are big, long things with nasty teeth.

As soon as the conger eel is in the rowing boat your guest is invited to toss it back out into the sea.

If you are actually going to try out this game why not sail out in separate rowing boats? It's safer for all concerned and it doesn't really matter then if your guests lose their nerve and end up with a flapping amphibian as an unwanted member of their crew.

If all else fails, stay on shore and enjoy a nice game of tiddlywinks.

Covewae Paella

This is a dish that originates from Spain, like bullfighting and tricky guitar playing. It wouldn't be unreasonable in the slightest to suggest the Spanish love their food but often can't be bothered to waste time preparing as they tend to sleep through most afternoons. This is the big difference between the Spanish and the French, who love preparing wonderful cuisine, oh and the fact they speak different languages.

So there's nothing fancy about Covewae Paella, it's nothing more than a bowl of fish of various varieties that all met an unfortunate end. No need to be choosy, just sling them in.

Paella originated in Valencia and consisted of fish, rice and saffron. Unfortunately we don't grow saffron on Covewae so we substitute it with lavender from the lower hills by our forest.

Fill a bowl with seawater.
Throw all sorts of things that once lived in the sea.
Add 2 or 3 sprigs of lavender
Bring to the boil.
Serve piping hot to your guest, although it isn't advisable to have a helping yourself as it tastes completely disgusting.
A meal guaranteed to get rid of unwanted guest.

Job done.

Crab Apple Sponge

A tasty pudding that's easy to prepare and one that's worthy of a not so tasty poem.

Pick an apple from a tree
Then pull a sponge out of the sea
In the rock pool find a crab
If you can't find one use a dab

Place them all upon a plate
An ideal dish if you're on a date
The easiest pudding of all time
And a way of writing a stupid rhyme

So there you have it. No sponge to cook in the usual way and no need to risk eating crab apples that aren't great for your stomach.

Atlantic Roll

One of the most popular puddings, particularly for children, is an Arctic Roll, a sponge filled with yummy ice-cream. Our Atlantic Roll bears no resemblance to such a treat whatsoever, but at least it's unique to our island.

Our version isn't so much a pudding but more a light afternoon snack, concocted by the fact that Covewae Island isn't anywhere near The Arctic but is surrounded by The Atlantic Ocean. Another factor is that it's usually too cold to eat ice-cream here so we prefer something more heart-warming to beat off the northern elements.

Prepare your Gaelic Bread.

Follow the directions found on the Gaelic Bread page.

Half fill a bucket with seawater.

Roll the bread in the water until it reaches a tacky consistency or until your hands are too cold to carry on kneading.

Light a small bonfire, nothing too extreme.

Place the mixture on a baking tray.

Bake the bread until golden brown.

Serve on its own or with a nice lump of cheese whilst watching a boring film on afternoon television.

More Jokes? Are you sure?

What would happen if a poisonous snake bit its lip whilst eating its dinner?

Would a potato make a successful detective if its eyes were peeled?

What do you call a carrot that has grown at right angles? A square root.

Does a banana wear its hair in bunches?

What does Covewae's police officer, Stuart, make to make you laugh? Tickled onions.

What was the snowman doing in the Covewae Island vegetable patch? It was picking its nose.

Who will you find camping on Covewae Island? Brussel scouts.

Did Elton John ever write a song called Soy Seems To Be The Hardest Word? Probably not, and we don't think he ever ate crocodile rock either.

What does Doctor Who love to eat? Dalek Bread.

Why should you never mix fruit with vegetables? Because it makes you feel melon-cauli.

Is a hedgehog's favourite fruit a spineapple?

If you make shoes out of banana skins have you made a pair of slippers?

Would a banana have to go to hospital if it wasn't peeling well?

If you spot a sausage coughing and spluttering along the road have you seen an old banger?

Are straw-berries a scarecrow's favourite meal?

Butter Scotch

We're not sure how to categorise this one as it seems to be caught between a pudding and an alcoholic treat. Either way, it's something we've tried to prepare on the island, but sadly with not too much success. You probably know why.

Take a slab of butter
And place it in a bowl
Then take a bottle of whiskey
And pour that in too, whole

Mix the butter and the Scotch
Until it makes a nice rich foam
Then take it out and drink it
If you're not driving home

Is this recipe a pudding?
Is this recipe a drink?
We're not too sure either
But at least it made you think

Battered Cod

Yet another fish dish from Covewae Island, hardly surprising as we're surrounded by water. Cod are a common species here, often seen swimming around just offshore. They as easy to catch as they are to prepare, as you will now discover.

Remove fishing tackle from your cupboard
Take your place on a rock
Cast your bait and wait for the rod to twitch
Begin bringing the captured cod to the shore making sure it passes over numerous small, jagged rocks.
Net the fish out of the water
Check it has been well battered
Fillet the fish, removing the head and the tail
Place in a baking tray on a smouldering fire
Cook for just 10 minutes
There is no need to cook in oil as all fish are full of their own oil anyway
Serve with a Covewae salad
Your easy to cook meal will prove to be a great success.
If not, throw it to the seagulls as they love a nice piece of cod.

Fishing Liners

What's the most intelligent fish that swims in the sea? A brain sturgeon.

Is a battle between two fish armies called tench warfare?

Which fish was dreaming of a white Christmas? Ling Crosby.

Are two angry dolphins talking at cross porpoises?

Was the fact that Noah only had two worms the reason he never took up fishing?

Where do fish sit in a line overnight? A carp ark.

Do fish keep their money in a riverbank?

A Tickleback is the fish that laughs the most.

Who are the most famous singing duo of all time? Pike and Tuna Turner.

Do all male fish swim around Covewae in search of a gillfriend?

If a monastery already has a fish friar do they need to find a chip monk?

How do you stop a fish from escaping? You fit a chub lock.

If a young dog is called a puppy then why aren't all young fish called guppies?

If you haven't seen a fish for a while it's always worth dropping them a line.

We've often wondered if all the fish around Scotland share the same surname of MacKerel.

Ravi-eel-i

Ravioli, a kind of baby-sized pillow-shaped pasta, was invented years ago by some Italian chef who had become bored with the boring helpings of spaghetti. His original idea was to fill the little pillows with either Italian cheese or minced meat. We on Covewae had another idea that proved it isn't only that cockney chaps that eat eels, jellied or otherwise.

Pasta itself is a simple food with the simple ingredients of flour, water and eggs that are all flattened to wafer thin strands. Ravioli looks different in its pillow form but it's made of the same stuff.

Eels are plentiful around Covewae but they're awkward to cook as long thin pans are a rarity and they only really fit into a baguette when cooked.

Here's a tip from Covewae. When you catch an eel if you place it on piece of newspaper it will stop wriggling, something to do with the print we think.

Catch an eel.
Slice the eel into small rounds, similar to the method of slicing a courgette.
Slice an onion into tiny pea-sized pieces.
Slice 2 tomatoes
Mix the ingredients and place them inside the pasta pillows.

Allow the bonfire to calm down so as not to burn the ingredients.

Cook slowly for around 8 to 10 minutes.

Sprinkle with chopped parsley.

Serve with a Covewae green salad.

As a mark of respect to the original dish, maybe serve with a white Italian wine. If you have no white Italian wine then make do with a nice cup of tea or orange squash.

Spratatouille

Inspired by ratatouille, a fine French delicacy of many centuries past, we present to you our own variation that we modified as a necessity due to the lack of ingredients such as aubergines, eggplants as they are known, and red peppers. Sprats are those little fish that swim around in their thousands upon thousands at a hundred miles per hour, thinking it keeps them safe when being attacked by the big monsters of the sea, from turtles to whales.

To the uninitiated, Sprats are often mistaken for sardines, to the point that they are often called sardines, but we on Covewae know better because they are not. A sprat is definitely a sprat and a sardine is definitely a sardine. We on the island both realise and respect the full potential of the diminutive sprat, particularly using the oil within its body as a cooking facility. It's saturated with the stuff and a passing shoal provides enough oil to keep us going in the kitchen for months.

Fry the sprats for literally 2 minutes.
Cut 6 cherry tomatoes into quarters and add to the mix.
Cut and slice an onion.
Slice courgettes, although small cucumbers will suffice.
Add the courgettes.

Stir the mixture and warm slowly so the onions remain crunchy and the tomato skins do not burn.

If there are no other herbs to hand then it's time to call in the bay leaves.

Sprinkle the bay leaves on the surface

Serve with a delightful Covewae green salad of water grasses and stems.

Unlike ratatouille, our Spratatouille is a main course meal in itself and not just a compliment to a meat dish.

The Pheasants Revolt

Although it verges on the politically incorrect these days, pheasant shooting still goes on in parts of the British countryside. We don't partake in such a pastime on Covewae Island and we don't have any roadkill to report as there are no vehicles on the island apart from an ancient land rover to round up the few sheep and goats we have here.

If a pheasant flies over from the mainland and dies of boredom, well that's another thing altogether.

Firstly, pluck the colourful feathers and keep them for numerous uses such as Christmas decorations, embellishing hats, writing like William Shakespeare used to scribe.

Having plucked the pheasant, add stuffing made from onions and beetroot, a Covewae Island delicacy if ever there was one and in keeping with the colourings of the bird.

Place baking tray on the bonfire with 3 or 4 sardines to produce an oily base.

Cook the pheasant slowly over 2 hours, turning every 20 minutes.

Once have turned every 20 minutes for no reason, turn the pheasant every 20 minutes too.

Peel potatoes.

Peel a variety of vegetables in preparation.

Place boiled potatoes in the same tray and let them crisp.

Boil mixed vegetables.

Serve in a similar way to a Sunday roast, at a well-place table.

A pheasant and delightful experience.

Anorak Potatoes

Of course you know all about jacket potatoes, but jackets give very little protection up in the northern regions where Covewae is situated. For that reason we had to come up with something that would keep potatoes warmer and that's what we did through our Anorak Potatoes recipe. So how does it work?

Put on your warmest anorak and make you way outdoors, taking a handful of potatoes with you.

Light the fire.

Peel the potatoes wearing gloves.

That's you wearing gloves and not the potatoes.

Bring a saucepan of seawater to the boil.

Add the potatoes and boil for 20 minutes.

Strain the water from the potatoes and place them in the pockets of your anorak.

They will stay warm until you are ready to serve.

Serve with whatever you choose.

Remember to clean your pockets the following day or the remains will stick to car keys and letters that need posting.

Olderberry Wine

Elderberry wine goes one step further on the island with the introduction of Olderberry Wine.

Elderberries are those little dark round things that grow on trees. The same can be said for our Olderberries.

Arm yourself with a shopping bag.

Visit as many fruit trees as you can.

You will find old fruit scattered around the ground, begging to be use in some way.

You may use apples, plums, pears, cherries and greengages, the squelchier the better.

Elderberries may be old but olderberries are obviously older and more bruised.

Throw all the fruit in a bucket and cover with a lid.

Let the fruits ferment for a few months, scraping off surface sediment once a month.

Store the juice in an old wine bottle.

Serve with your favourite meal.

Be warned, it will probably taste disgusting but, hey, at least you made it yourself with fruit that well passed their 'best before' date.